Badger the Mystical Mutt

and the Bigfoot Brigade

McNicol Jackson

JF

THE LUNICORN PRESS
Glasgow
Text © Lyn McNicol and Laura Cameron Jackson 2015
Illustrations © Laura Cameron Jackson 2015
All rights reserved

First published 2015 by The Lunicorn Press
1

Printed by Martins the Printers, Berwick-upon-Tweed
Designed and typeset by Heather MacPherson at Raspberry
Creative Type
Set in 14.25 pt Gentium Book

British Library Cataloguing in Publication Data
A CIP catalogue record for this book is available from the British
Library

ISBN: 978-0-9929264-0-3

www.badgerthemysticalmutt.com
www.facebook.com/badgermutt
www.twitter.com/badgermutt

For Miss Monaghan and Becca Houston

Praise for the first series
of *Badger the Mystical Mutt*

"A fun, fast-paced romp of a read for younger readers ... terrific stuff!"
Cathy Cassidy

"Pitch-perfect subtlety and wit."
Shari Low

"Badger the Mystical Mutt has quickly become a firm favourite with children beginning to read on their own."
Off the Page, Stirling Book Festival

"Badger does help bring a smile to your face with his unusual approach to magic making."
Missing Sleep

"There are some underlying morality themes that should allow vigorous class discussions."
Stephen King, The School Librarian Magazine

"Once again McNicol & Jackson have come up with a brilliant story where Badger and his mystical powers are called upon to help out his friends."
BFK Books

"Kids' book takes world by storm."
The Scottish Sun

"Cue another dog-tastic tale of friendship, adversity and wonky magic."
The Daily Record

"A moving and joyful story which warmed the heart of this cynical old journalist."
That's Books

"First-time winner."
The Evening Times

"A toast-loving, magical hound, who has been winning fans in book shops, libraries and schools across Scotland."
The List

"A charming and very funny children's story."
Diana Cooper

"McNicol & Jackson have created a charming new book character; a toast-crunching hound named Badger."
Aye Write, Glasgow's Book Festival

"A truly magical story which has all the hallmarks of a future children's classic!"
Ursula James

"Badger the Mystical Mutt is the coolest doggie around and in his brilliant stories he helps young kids understand their world and believe in themselves and their ambitions."
Vegetarian Living Magazine

Prologue

Badger the Mystical Mutt pressed the cruise control button on the dashboard of his ancient travelling machine, the Wim-Wim for a Wowser. He sighed happily and sat back with his paws behind his head.

The sun shone, the clouds had scarpered, and he had a tower of hot, buttered toast stashed for the journey. All was well, and he now had some much deserved time off.

Badger had barely closed his eyes when something shot into the cockpit of the Wim-Wim. He jumped, and opened one eye warily to see a perfectly folded envelope fluttering next to him. It was addressed to Badger the Mystical Mutt and the words "Mission Statement" were stamped across it in bright red ink.

It looks like I'm back on duty sooner than I thought. He felt the familiar badgical-magical thrill of adventure and carefully opened the envelope. Two pieces of paper fell out. One was a note from Captain Bravebark, his ancestor in the Ring of Brodgar. It read:

To the Heralayan Mountain, you must hurry, where the ground is deep in snow. Seek Twin Pines amidst the flurry. You'll find it in a glow.

Badger was baffled. He scratched his head and read on.

Inside Twin Pines, a family lives in constant worry. The headline will tell you all you need to know.

Badger frowned, and looked at the other piece of paper. It was a newspaper cutting from the *Paws of the World;* a notorious publication run by Schubert Furdog, leader of the infamous news hounds: the Pupparazzi. He shuddered and peered at the headline emblazoned across the top of the page, it said:

THE HUNT IN THE HERALAYAN MOUNTAIN CONTINUES: WE ARE ONE STEP CLOSER TO CATCHING THE BIGFOOT MONSTER.

Next to the article was a blurry photograph of a large, furry figure, which was captioned *"Official Bigfoot Sighting"*.

Badger shook his head in puzzlement and shivered excitedly. He knew where he had to go. He switched off the cruise control on the Wim-Wim, set its navigation system for the Heralayan Mountain, and pushed the throttle to full thrust.

He was on his way.

Chapter One

"Wooooooah!" yelled Badger the Mystical Mutt, shaking a heap of snow from his head. "Where did *that* come from?"

In the distance, he heard a giggle. His eyes darted around nervously. He stood very still, listening to the silence and shivering, the cold snow of the Heralayan Mountain on his paws. He looked back to where he had parked his trusty Wim-Wim at the start of his mission. It glowed and winked at the foot of the mountain by the biggest pine tree on the slopes.

Surely not, thought Badger, *how could the Wim-Wim throw a snowball?*

He looked ahead at the snow-covered peaks. *Splat!* Another snowball and another giggle.

Giggling snowballs? Whatever next?

He wiped the last of the dripping snow
from his fur and jumped when he heard
another muffled giggle and then the crunch
of footsteps upon the snow. He sensed
that he was not alone, but he knew he had
to carry on. He'd been trudging through
snowdrift after snowdrift for what seemed

like days. He shielded his eyes against the low-lying sun and realised he had, in fact, probably only trudged for an hour. But his paws were heavy from ploughing through the crisp snow, and his toes were freezing cold.

He sniffed the cold air and patted his tummy. In the excitement of the trip, he'd forgotten to pack his knapsack full of his favourite snack — toast — and had left it behind in the Wim-Wim. His stomach rumbled noisily in the eerie hush of the white-out. He shook his head and unfolded a tiny piece of paper. He read the mission statement aloud again.

Seek Twin Pines amidst the flurry. You'll find it in a glow.

He scratched his head and scanned the skyline. He could see plenty of trees. In fact, *all* he could see were the peaks of hundreds of pine trees peeking through the snow.

Finding Twin Pines amongst this lot wasn't going to be easy.

Ahead he saw a few branches shake off their snow dust and heard a thud. Badger gulped.

Is hunger making me imagine things because I'm sure those branches just moved?

He gave himself a blustery shake and plodded on, muttering a hurried plea to his magic red-and-white polka-dot neckerchief:

"'Chief, 'Chief, my friend and saviour,
Please do for me this little favour.

*Set me on the
proper track
To fill my tummy
with a snack."*
The neckerchief
unfurled from
Badger's neck
and pointed east.
The Mystical
Mutt followed the
direction of his guide
and spied a set of giant
footprints ahead of him. He
rummaged in his knapsack and pulled
out a magnifying glass. He peered at the
footprints, which were now even more
gigantic.

Aha, as I thought! I'm not alone after all.

He sniffed the ground with great
concentration, and continued on. He'd been
to the Heralayan Mountain before, but
never in winter, and never this far in.

His excellent travelling machine, The
Wim-Wim for a Wowser to Wind the
Weather up on a Wet Day, ran on Haboba

juice. The most essential and rarest ingredient of Haboba juice was the burp of a big-footed Yeti. In return for a barrel of raspberry and Brussels-sprout lemonade — guaranteed to make burps of the burpiest kind – Badger usually met his Yeti friend at the big pine tree at the bottom of the mountain. But not today!

His mission seemed to be taking him deeper into the forest. He sighed and carried on.

Suddenly, the snow whirled into a fierce blizzard and

a mashing, thrashing and crunching clatter surrounded him. A pack of vicious hounds appeared, seemingly out of nowhere, pulling a toboggan.

Uh oh, are these the dreaded Pupparazzi: the privacy robbers? He sighed.

The loudest of the hounds stepped forward and announced himself: "I'm Schubert Furdog, head reporter of the *Paws of the World* newspaper, and these are my news hounds, the Pupparazzi photographers.

Badger froze, as he was jostled by cameras whirring and telescopic lenses poking and prodding him on the nose. He swatted away one of the Pupparazzi, who was particularly interested in taking pictures of the tuft on top of his head.

This is feeling a teensy weensy bit uncomfortable, winced Badger, trying to remove a camera lens from his ear.

In the midst of the mayhem, Badger noticed one of the news hounds standing away from the group. He stood quietly next

to the toboggan, watching and writing in his notebook. He seemed different from the others, taller and more elegant. He wore a long red and blue scarf with green fringes and carried a satchel over his shoulder.

As one of the Pupparazzi tried to photograph the entire contents of Badger's knapsack, Schubert suddenly shouted over the noise:

"You are a stranger on this snow, so declare your business here immediately."

Badger grinned sheepishly, looked bravely at the motley crew and said, "Me? Oh ... erm ... I'm just out for a stroll."

"Nonsense!" barked Schubert, "No one, neither man nor beast, comes to these parts just for a *stroll*. Now what's your real reason for being here?"

Thinking on his paws, Badger replied quickly. "Actually, I'm a champion snowboarder. I was told that the powder here is the most challenging in the world."

"Snowboarding, eh? Then where's your board? Where's your gear?" growled Schubert suspiciously.

Badger looked around him, and noticed one of the news hounds on his tummy taking close-up pictures of his paws, as another laid a tape measure against his toes.

"My Sherpas are arriving later with all that," he fibbed. "I decided to take a look at the slopes first. Er, excuse me," asked Badger looking down at the newshounds crawling around by his feet. "Do you mind telling me exactly what you are doing?"

"We're looking for Big Feet: one particular very Big Foot in fact, but yours don't measure up, so you're free to go," snarled Schubert.

"Thank you," said Badger, "but I'm a bit lost and I haven't eaten for ages. Do you have any suggestions where I might find some hot, buttered toast?"

Schubert smirked and pointed further up the mountain.

"You could try Miss Monaghan's shop, but she's a fiend with her shutter, so if you're not fast, you're last. Okay, be on your way, but I'll be expecting to see some magnificent crust-bustin' from you on the piste. Remember ... I'm watching you," said Schubert, pointing his paws to his eyes and back to Badger.

The Pupparazzi took more sideways pictures of snowflakes, icicles and Badger's footprints. The news hound with the long scarf and the satchel hadn't moved at all. He raised his paw in a silent salute to Badger.

Schubert Furdog gestured for his Pupparazzi news hounds to retreat and they disappeared as quickly as they had materialised.

Badger breathed a grateful sigh of relief. He trembled at the thought of meeting the hounds again, and shuddered at the very idea of snowboarding at speed anywhere, let alone here. He shook himself again, and with a desperate need for toast hiked onwards.

The footprints he'd been following had been trampled by the news hounds. He sniffed the air deeply to catch the scent of the trail again.

Up ahead he spotted a solitary shack with smoke coming out of its tiny chimney.

Hurrah! That must be Miss Monaghan's. Toast is within my sights at last. He trekked faster towards the kiosk.

But inside the shack, a haughty mountain goat called Miss Monaghan had already seen the Mystical Mutt approach.

Badger reached Miss Monaghan's counter. His eyes widened at the array of bits and bobs and foodstuffs on her shelves. He spotted Crunchy Munchy Chewy Chops, Buddy Bites and a sign advertising hot, buttered and fully filled toasties. All of a sudden, a wooden shutter crashed down on the counter and closed the hatch.

The shutter caught the end of Badger's
neckerchief, leaving the mutt stuck, face-
down, trapped on the outside ledge.

"Who are you, and what do you want?"
shouted an angry voice from inside.

Before Badger could answer, his head battered against the shutter, as his neckerchief was tugged sharply from the other side. With his nose wedged against the kiosk, he pleaded for mercy.

"Please, Miss Monaghan, I'm Badger the Mystical Mutt and I only want some toast. I've been travelling for ages. I'm very hungry and now I've got a sore nose as well."

"The famous Badger the Mystical Mutt, you say? I don't believe you. You must be an imposter, otherwise, you'd use your magic to free yourself," said Miss Monaghan yanking his neckerchief again.

He groaned and mustered up his remaining energy.

"'Chief, 'Chief, fly into the shack,
Look around and find me a snack."

Badger's neckerchief unfurled from his neck and whizzed under the shutter. On the other side, Miss Monaghan was in a tizzy as 'Chief flew backwards and forwards, upwards and downwards, and spun around her head.

The shutter shot up.

"Okay, okay, I believe you. Now, get this fluttering flying thing out of my shop,"

screeched Miss Monaghan, swiping wildly at 'Chief.

"Not before I feed my tummy, Miss Monaghan," laughed Badger.

"Take this and be gone!" offered the goat, throwing a goat's cheese and pine nut toastie across the counter.

"Thank you," said Badger, *"'Chief, 'Chief, please leave the shack, for I now have my toastastic snack."*

Miss Monaghan wiped her counter clean of crumbs and was about to pull her shutter down again when Badger placed his paws on the counter and said: "Just one other thing, Miss Monaghan ..."

The goat looked at Badger warily.

"Can you tell me where Twin Pines is, please?"

"Why do you want to know?" asked Miss Monaghan suspiciously.

"I've been sent on a mission to help those who live there."

"As long as you're truly here to help, Badger, and since your reputation is one of bravery and goodness, head along there and you'll find it. But be careful. The family are good friends of mine, and they are being hunted down by those who know no better. They only wish to live in peace. I hope you *can* help them," smiled Miss Monaghan, pointing ahead.

Then the shutter came down.

As Badger plodded on, dusk was falling. Somewhere in the distance he could see two pine trees standing alone, and there was definitely a glow.

Chapter Two

"*Magenta polenta and curried pip steaks;*
A sachet of aubergine domino flakes;
Butter cream icing on jangle flub cakes;
This is the dinner for Badger, I'll make"
A large furry beast, with a bright white
apron, fussed around her kitchen, singing

merrily, with mixing bowls, spatulas, wooden spoons, frying pans, jam jars, pots and a set of scales.

The fire was roaring.

Badger followed the glow. He spotted footsteps again, along the trail weaving through the trees, towards a path of pine-tree bark. Then he heard the crush of snow moving underfoot nearby, followed by a fit of giggles.

Uh oh, thought Badger, *I feel a snowball coming on.*

Splat! Cold, wet snow soaked his neckerchief as two small creatures fell out of a tree, laughing and rolling around.

"Oi!" said Badger, watching the two bundles of fur covered in snow.

"Oi, indeed!" shouted a big voice as an even bigger bundle of fur swept the two little ones off the ground and held them in mid-air. They squirmed and squealed in delight.

"We knew you were coming and just wanted to welcome you. I'm Flossy," announced the smaller of the two furry bundles proudly, "and this is my brother, Bossie. We're soooooooo excited!"

"We're never allowed any visitors and we're not supposed to go outside. It's so boring," added Bossie quietly. "So, seeing you is an epic treat for us."

"You're not supposed to be out!" said the huge furry creature sternly. "You *know* how dangerous it can be." He dropped them both onto the soft snow.

Badger grinned to see his old friend again.

"Well, hello, Mr Bigfoot. I didn't know it was you I was meeting at Twin Pines. A badgical-magical hello to you too, Flossy and Bossie. I was sent vague instructions, but no names. I'm so glad it's you, Mr Bigfoot. How are you?" said Badger.

"Sorry about that. Information is on a need-to-know basis with us," said Mr Bigfoot. "We're very pleased you made it. But where is that Wim-Wam flying thing of yours?"

"Wim-Wim," grinned Badger, "I had to park it at the bottom of the mountain. There are too many trees further up for a good landing. I travelled the rest of the way by paw."

"Okay," said Mr Bigfoot, "as long as you remember where you left it. When the snow falls, it covers everything. Right, we really do need your help. Follow me."

Mr Bigfoot, Badger, Flossy and Bossie all headed up the pine-tree-bark path, towards the glow of Twin Pines. Although Badger had met Mr Bigfoot before, he had never seen his family or visited his home.

"Welcome to our humble abode," said Mr Bigfoot, flinging open the large wooden door of his house.

"Look who I found?" he bellowed to his wife. "Badger the Mystical Mutt and these two ragamuffins."

"Not again, you two! How many times have I told you not to play outdoors?" sighed Mrs Bigfoot, shaking her head at her children. "Now, go and get cleaned up. Badger, I'm delighted to meet you, I have heard all about you and your mystical ways." Mrs Bigfoot pulled Badger into a giant Yeti hug.

"Oh my goodness! Is that magenta polenta I can smell?" said Badger sniffing the freshly baking aromas.

Mrs Bigfoot smiled widely, and nodded proudly. "Mr Bigfoot told me it was one of your favourites."

"And if I'm not mistaken, I'm also catching the distinct scent of some jangle flub cakes?" said Badger inhaling deeply.

"Right again! Now, come on in, and let's get you dry. How long has it been since you were last at the mountain?"

"Not since the last time I topped up the Wim-Wim, Mrs Bigfoot, which must have been about twenty past the last century?"

Mrs Bigfoot smiled and ushered Badger inside, nervously scanning the landscape behind her.

"Did anyone follow you?" she asked anxiously.

"No, but I did meet some odd characters on my way. He said his name was Schubert Furdog and his hounds were the Pupparazzi. Do you know them?"

"Oh no," groaned Mr Bigfoot, "I'm afraid we do, only too well. Let's get you settled and fed and then I'll be back shortly to tell you all about them. I'm sorry to leave again, after you've just arrived, but there's something I must get from Miss Monaghan's before she shuts her shutter."

"Good luck with that," said Badger settling down in front of the cosy fire, as Mr Bigfoot headed back into the snowy terrain.

The little Bigfoots trundled noisily downstairs, freshly washed and in their pyjamas. They pounced on their visitor excitedly.

"Woah!" said Badger, straightening his neckerchief "Could you possibly be the same two snowball tossing scamps, I met earlier?"

Mrs Bigfoot shouted through from the kitchen: "Leave Badger alone. He's had a big journey to get here and will be tired."

Badger grinned, gave them each a high five and announced: "Luckily for you two, I come bearing no grudges for the snowballs, only gifts."

Badger hurriedly tapped his neckerchief and asked for some assistance. He held his paws behind his back and hoped that 'Chief had been able to deliver.

"Pick a paw," teased Badger.

Immediately, Flossy said "I'll have your left paw please, Badger!"

Badger squirmed, and produced his left paw, hoping to goodness that it wasn't empty. As he unfurled his paw, Flossy screamed. There, in his palm, was a shiny pink yo-yo.

"Oh thank you, Badger. You're the best guest we've had at Twin Pines, ever."

Bossie pointed to Badger's right paw. The Mystical Mutt revealed a rainbow-coloured spinning top.

"Wow!" said Bossie "Thank you, Mister Badger. That's amazing."

Badger sat back and relaxed as the little Bigfoots played with their new toys.

Mrs Bigfoot appeared from the kitchen with a tray of treats and snacks. Badger

drooled and all thoughts of Schubert
Furdog, the news hounds and the trek in the
snow left him as he tucked into the delicious
feast in front of him.

Chapter Three

Badger dozed contentedly snuggled in the sofa. He was full after his meal and was dreaming of ripping flakes on an easy-peasy cruiser-run in the snow, on his board. His paws were tied tightly to the stomp pads, and he was slaloming, corkscrewing and showing off with tail wheelies. Then all at once, he went *boomph* and face-planted rapidly into deep snow. He awoke with a shiver.

There, in front of him, was Mr Bigfoot, home from his trip to the shop.

"Hello again, old friend," said Mr Bigfoot, taking the box of groceries into the kitchen. "You've had your fill of Mrs Bigfoot's famous magenta polenta then?"

"Yes" sighed Badger, "It was lip-smacking-tastic, thank you."

"I hope you haven't brought any more raspberry and Brussels-sprout lemonade. I'm all out of burps tonight." Mr Bigfoot sat down on the armchair, and started to heave at his almighty boots.

"No. I was summoned here on an entirely different mission. Hopefully, one which will help you? I hear there's trouble afoot."

"Yes, we did ask for help, so your visit is very timely. Thank you for coming. It's been quite an ordeal," frowned Mr Bigfoot.

Badger moved closer to hear more, but was interrupted.

"Dad, you're home!" yelled the children leaping on top of him.

"Aha, my lovelies, I have treats for you: a bag of bon-bons. Flossy, you've got strawberry fizzlewhizz, and Bossie, you have lemon tangyfang. I just caught Miss Monaghan's shop before she closed."

"Yum yum!" squealed Flossy and Bossie together, grabbing the bags and disappearing behind the sofa.

"You've just had your dinner," said Mrs Bigfoot. "Put them aside for later."

"And for you, my dear Mrs Bigfoot, there's a spray of giant hogweed, cartwheel flowers and cow parsnips on the kitchen table," offered Mr Bigfoot sweetly.

"Thank you, twinkle toes. Now did you remember to get me some more domino flakes from Mrs Monaghan's? They were on my shopping list," beamed Mrs Bigfoot.

"Oops, honey bunch, I forgot. Sorry." Mr Bigfoot rolled his eyes at Badger.

"Have you met Miss Monaghan, Badger?" asked Mrs Bigfoot mischievously.

"I did indeed. She was a little gruff with me."

Mrs Bigfoot guffawed loudly. "That's one way to describe her. She's very protective of us all. She's like a nanny to Flossy and Bossie. I *do* miss our weekly chats."

"Don't you see her when you go for your shopping?" asked Badger.

"I'm afraid not. It's just not safe for me to go there at the moment," said Mrs Bigfoot sadly. "I can't even go and choose new thimbles and threads for darning Mr Bigfoot's socks."

"Because of Schubert Furdog and his Pupparazzi?" asked Badger.

Mrs Bigfoot nodded.

"As much as she does her best to look out for us, none of us can really risk popping into Miss Monaghan's for a weekly shop. The Pupparazzi have got the place surrounded. I do try when I know the hounds are elsewhere, but it's tricky," admitted Mr Bigfoot.

Badger watched wide-eyed,
as Mr Bigfoot pulled off his
huge boots, followed by
a pair of stripy woollen
socks covered in bright red
pom-poms. Badger raised
his eyebrows as Mr Bigfoot
removed yet another layer of
bright blue fluffy socks. He
then untied several hot water
bottles before taking off a pair
of ziggy-zaggy patterned socks
and patchwork cushioned pads,
two pink legwarmers, and more
socks until, eventually, Badger saw
Mr Bigfoot's bare and *tiny* feet.

"Wow!" said Badger. "Are those really your feet?"

Mr Bigfoot placed his massive boots by the fire, and hung all his socks in a row, as Flossy and Bossie returned with a basin of hot, steaming water. He eased his feet into the basin and sighed.

"They are indeed. You see, Badger," he said wearily, "I don't actually have big feet, or even *a* big foot. It's all a myth. I am being chased and hounded as this terrible monster, Bigfoot, but I've got very small feet and really big bunions. And they're really very, very sore."

44

Chapter Four

Badger slept fitfully, worried about his friend Mr Bigfoot and his agonising bunions, as well as his wife, Mrs Bigfoot, and their children, Flossy and Bossie. He awoke with a start. But all was quiet within Twin Pines. He rolled over and tried to go back to sleep.

Mrs Bigfoot was already up and in the kitchen preparing breakfast. Mr Bigfoot was long gone on his daily hunt for food for his family.

Unable to sleep, Badger got up and joined Mrs Bigfoot downstairs.

"I'm sorry to ask you, Mrs Bigfoot, but can you tell me all about Schubert Furdog and his hounds. Is now a good time?"

Mrs Bigfoot sat down wearily at the kitchen table and sighed.

"Badger, we are just an everyday family of Yetis, but because there are very few of us left on this planet, the outside world is making it their business to hunt us down. The children can't go outside to play; Mr Bigfoot is constantly covering his tracks; and, as you know, I can't even pop into Miss Monaghan's for my weekly grocery shop."

"That's awful," said Badger. "How do the children cope with playing indoors all the time? And more to the point, how do you cope relying on Mr Bigfoot to get everything on your shopping list, especially when he's risking being seen by doing so?"

"Well, we get by with the shopping, and Mr Bigfoot is good at outsmarting Schubert and his news hounds, but it's the children I worry about most. They need to play in the snow, on the slopes and be outdoors, but those dreaded Pupparazzi just won't allow it."

"How does Mr Bigfoot manage to dodge them so well?" asked Badger

"He has a few snow tricks, but they don't always work, and sometimes the news hounds catch a glimpse of him and go into a frenzy. You see, they think none of the Big Folk believe we actually exist, and they are desperate to prove the Big Folk wrong."

"I can sympathise with his tricks going awry," smiled Badger. "I'm not the best at magic myself."

Mrs Bigfoot looked at Badger in shock.

"But, Badger, I thought you were the one who could come and put a stop to all this! We asked for help, and were told you were the one to help us. What do you mean your magic doesn't always work?"

Badger grabbed another slice of hot, buttered toast from the bread board and grinned hopefully.

"I'm sure I *can* help. Trust me. I *am* the Mystical Mutt, after all."

Mrs Bigfoot smiled anxiously.

Λ loud knock at the door made them both jump, followed by a commotion outside. Camera flashes lit up the room.

"Oh no," said Mrs Bigfoot in a panic "Schubert and his Pupparazzi must have found out where we live. Children, quick, hide!"

"Uh oh, keep calm!" said Badger bravely. "All we need is a spell to get rid of them. Let's gather round the table and stay really quiet."

Mrs Bigfoot, Flossy and Bossie did as they were told.

"Mrs Bigfoot, do you have a mixing bowl, some icing sugar, a coconut, a whisk, and some cinnamon, please?"

Mrs Bigfoot flung open her kitchen cupboards in a panic, searching for the ingredients required by the Mystical Mutt. She placed the bowl and all of the items in front of Badger. Sparkles of light appeared as he began to stir the mix.

"Now, this should make them all just ... erm ... float away from the door." Badger's eyebrows twitched as he uttered the spell:

"Twirly-whirly snowflakes and cinnamon spice,
Dance yourself dizzy on coconut ice,
Pink sugar moonbeams and marshmallow pies,
All spinning round in front of our eyes."

Flossy, Bossie and Mrs Bigfoot looked on in wonder at the Mystical Mutt making his magic. They held their breath. Suddenly they felt themselves being lifted up and began hovering around the room. *Boom!* The ingredients blasted into the air.

"It's raining marshmallows!" yelled Flossy, spinning around the kitchen table

with her tongue sticking out to catch the fluffy sweetness.

"It doesn't appear to have gone *quite* as I had planned. It was supposed to work with that lot outdoors, not *us*," yelled Badger, hanging onto his chair.

Amidst the hullabaloo, the door banged louder.

"What's going on in there?" cried a voice from outside.

"This calls for Plan B!" shrieked Badger, who was now covered in a sticky, sumptuous mess.

"What's that then?" shouted the three Bigfoots.

"I'm still figuring it out," grinned Badger awkwardly. "Stay there!"

Badger let go of the chair and landed on the floor with a bump. He staggered dizzily to the front door and poked his head out. On the doorstep stood a fox in a trilby, carrying a bulging rucksack, stuffed full of knick-knacks.

"Oh hullo, mate. I just need to get some new pictures of the crew for my merchandise."

"Who are *you*?" asked Badger in
bewilderment.

"I'm Shifty Sid, sir, at your service, for
all your merchandise needs," bowed the
fox "Are they in? Who are *you* anyway? And
why are you covered in marshmallows?
Have I missed a party?"

"Ah," said Badger, noticing a window open to his left. "Not at all. We were just ... erm ... making some coconut ices." He licked his lips.

Mrs Bigfoot appeared by his side and said: "What have I told you about coming to the house, Sid?"

"I know, Mrs Bigfoot, but I'm all out of stock. The Pupparazzi have gone mad for the new range of Bigfoot key rings, and the tourists have ordered loads of t-shirts this year. I just need some new photographs for the website," smiled Shifty Sid charmingly.

"I thought we said no more photographs, Sid," sighed Mrs Bigfoot.

"I know, but business is booming." He shrugged.

Suddenly, they all heard a yell.

"*Snowballs awaaaaaaaaaaaaaaaaaaaaaaay!*"

The branches above Twin Pines shook vigorously as an avalanche of snow fell directly onto Shifty Sid, turning him into a living snowman. Snowballs whizzed past the door. Badger and Mrs Bigfoot looked at the white-out chaos outside and spotted Flossy and Bossie hanging upside down from the branch, giggling.

"Right, you two, inside now!" ordered Mrs Bigfoot sternly.

Badger popped a carrot into Shifty Sid's mouth, and three pebbles in his belly. "No photos today, *mate*," he said, and promptly shut the door.

Inside, after Mrs Bigfoot had banished Flossy and Bossie upstairs to sulk, she sat down heavily at the kitchen table.

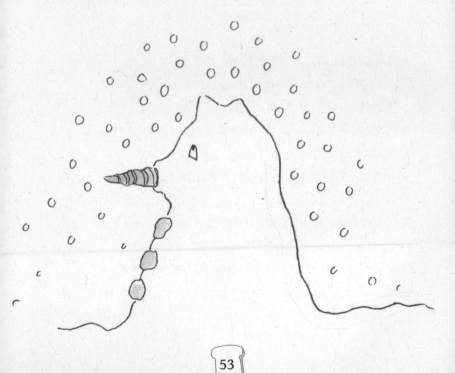

"At least it wasn't Schubert and his news hounds. Shifty Sid has been making a living selling all sorts of bric-a-brac with the Bigfoot name for years. He's an honest scallywag, a lovable rogue. I don't want to see him go out of business." She sighed.

"Okay, well, present situation averted," said Badger, "Meanwhile, I need to go after Mr Bigfoot. Where does he usually go on his foraging?"

"He always heads off in the direction of the Velvet Road, towards the Kora La, then onto Pookamoa."

Badger scratched his head and asked: "I don't suppose you have directions?"

Mrs Bigfoot chuckled. "I have an old-fashioned map, if that will help." She unfurled a big old cloth map of the ancient area and placed it on the table.

"It's difficult to navigate when the peaks are so full of snow. You'll need to be careful Badger. The Velvet Road winds across this mountain. Once you are through the trees, you will come to some huge rocks, carved

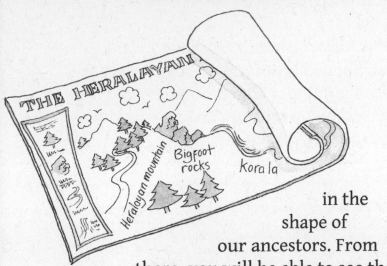

in the
shape of
our ancestors. From
there, you will be able to see the
Kora La waterfall splashing down into
the streams that lead through the land to
Pookamoa."

Badger peered in awe at the map laid out
on the table, then tapped his neckerchief
and whispered:

"*Show koo ray, my chief and guide,*
Take me where Mr Bigfoot hides."

Badger's neckerchief unfurled from his
neck and pointed towards the door. Badger
snatched a final slice of toast and followed.

Outside, 'Chief flew north, and Badger
ran to catch up. The Mystical Mutt stopped
and caught his breath. Then he had a better

idea. He straightened his legs, spun his tail, flapped his ears, hovered shakily in the air, and took flight. Soon, he and his neckerchief were high and side by side in the snow-laden sky.

Mr Bigfoot was already at Pookamoa, with a hefty catch of fish, when Schubert and his news hounds arrived.

Chapter Five

"Gotcha, at last!" screeched Schubert
excitedly. "You big hairy lump, I've been
after you for years, and now here you are,
right in front of me. What a story this will
make. I can see the headlines and the front
pages now."

Mr Bigfoot shielded his eyes from the
persistent snap and flash of the cameras
and scanned around for an escape route,
but the news hounds had him completely
surrounded.

He lunged forward and roared at them
wildly. And then everything went black.

Badger watched in horror from above as
his friend slumped to the ground with
a massive thud. He could see the tail-end
of a dart embedded in Mr Bigfoot's
neck.

"Right, quick," ordered the leader of the Pupparazzi, pointing at the motionless pile of fur. "That has stunned him for a few minutes at most. Tie him up before he wakens."

The news hounds put down their cameras and dragged chains from their toboggan.

Badger panicked. He had to help his friend, and quickly. For once, he managed to land quietly, some way off from the kerfuffle.

I need to pinch their cameras before they notice, then divert their attention, he thought.

Suddenly the news hounds jumped back in alarm, as an almighty rumble of a snore vibrated through the Kora La, and down the Velvet Road.

"Hurry up! He's still fast asleep," barked Schubert, "but we don't have long before the stun dart wears off."

Badger racked his brains for the perfect spell. And then he remembered his hypnotic robotic spell!

With a little help from his neckerchief, he could capture them all and free his friend.

He bounded over to Schubert and the news hounds and tapped his neckerchief.

"We really must stop bumping into each other like this," said Badger amiably.

"You again? The snowboarding champ? We're a bit busy at the moment, so why don't you run along and slide down some slopes or something?"

The news hounds gathered around Schubert and growled at Badger. But one, Badger noticed, didn't come forward: the one with the scarf and the satchel.

"What's that?" Badger pointed at the snoring Mr Bigfoot.

"What's what?" asked Schubert, who was visibly annoyed.

Badger's neckerchief unravelled from his neck and took the shape of a pendulum with a double knot at the bottom. It swung gently from side to side. Badger looked directly at Schubert, and then at the news hounds. He beckoned for them all to come closer and whispered:

"Look at this knot swinging to and fro.
See how it dangles above the snow.
Now you feel sleepy, and a little hypnotic.
Whenever you move, it will be quite robotic.
You will now do as I advise.
Look into my eyes ... look into my eyes."

Schubert and his hounds stood mesmerised, slack-jawed and still. Badger continued.

*"I'll be your master. When I count to three
You will undo the chains and set my friend free.
Then I will show you your best story yet
But all that you see, you will quickly forget"*

Badger clicked his paws and counted: one, two and three. Schubert and his hounds stood to immediate attention.

Mr Bigfoot groaned and grunted; he was beginning to wake up.

"Go and unchain him," commanded Badger. The news hounds moved mechanically to release their prisoner.

Mr Bigfoot pulled the dart out of his neck and shook himself.

"What's happening, Badger? I thought they'd finally caught me, and I'd never see Mrs Bigfoot and Flossy and Bossie again."

"Ah," said Badger. "I'm afraid it's only temporary. I've hypnotised them for the time being. There is one word which will act as a trigger, to bring them out of the trance, I've just got to make sure I don't say it ... yet."

"What is it?" asked Mr Bigfoot.

"I can't tell you because I can't say it aloud or we'll be in trouble. Why don't you head back to Twin Pines and take cover? I'm going to take this lot on a trip they'll never forget."

Although they will forget it, ultimately, Badger remembered.

"Oh, one more thing before you go" said Badger, "grab their cameras and delete all the pictures of you, or bury their rolls of film somewhere they will never be found."

"Good plan, Badger. I'm on it."

Then Badger pointed up the mountain, where a sumptuous thick red carpet was unrolling its way downwards.

Chapter Six

The end of the red carpet came to rest at Badger's feet. He rounded up the Pupparazzi and got them into a line.

"Schubert, you and your hounds follow my lead. We're following the red carpet to the top of the mountain."

The pack marched in formation obediently behind Badger.

The weight of the carpet had flattened the snow underfoot making the ascent easier, but Badger was still out of puff. He was in need of a snack to boost his energy, but once again, he hadn't packed any provisions.

Finally, he could see the summit ahead. They plodded on.

The carpet ended at an entrance with a sign on it saying "Stage Door". Badger

turned the handle apprehensively,
wondering what could possibly be on the
other side.

The door swung open. There, in front of
him, on the other side of the door, hung a

big, fluffy white cloud.

"You took your time, Badger! I've been hanging around for ages," said his old friend, Nippy Nimbus, the grumpiest cloud in the world.

"I wondered when I'd see you again, Nippy. I would have been much quicker if I'd had some toast in my tummy."

Just then, a rumpus kicked off behind him.

"Duh!" groaned Badger, putting his head in his paws, "I said *toast.*"

"No problem there, surely! You live, breathe and sleep higgledy-piggledy towers of toast, so what's wrong with saying it?" asked Nippy.

"I know," said Badger looking at the snarling news hounds and their leader, "but the word 'toast' was the trigger to bring them all out of the trance, and stop them being robotic and obeying my every command."

"Uh oh!" shrugged Nippy, "You're on your own with this then. Good luck!"

Schubert strode up to Badger angrily.

"You again! What are we doing here? And why are we following *you;* a snowboarder?"

"Ah," said Badger, "that's because I've got a great story for you."

"We're already on the trail of a great story: the best one ever actually," said Schubert snootily. "We are close to catching the elusive Yeti; the most abominable snowman of all: Bigfoot. So, back off!"

"Erm, it's actually *Mr* Bigfoot, but he's not here, so you're wasting your time," said Badger casually.

"But I distinctly remember seeing him." Schubert scratched his head.

"You must have dreamt it then, because I can assure you, you're barking up the wrong tree. But," said Badger majestically, "I *can* introduce you to a living unicorn, if you follow me."

"A unicorn? What nonsense! Everyone knows that unicorns are mythical beasts."

"Well, it's your loss, if you don't want to

find out. But what a scoop for you, if I'm telling the truth!"

Badger turned his back on Schubert and the Pupparazzi who were deep in conference about what to do next. Badger winked at Nippy and whispered: "They don't actually remember capturing Mr Bigfoot, so at least that bit of my hypnotic robotic spell worked."

"Superb! Give yourself a pat on the back for that then, Badger," sneered Nippy. "But you still need the password to get through me, to the Enchanted Forest."

Badger smiled and produced a card from under his neckerchief.

"I don't need a password today because I've got *this* instead: a press pass," beamed Badger proudly.

Nippy peered at the lettering and photograph on the card and grumbled: "Okay, jump on. After all, a press pass gives you immediate access to all areas, but you mark my words, it's for *today* only."

Badger leapt onto the cantankerous

cloud, and shouted over to Schubert. "Well, are you coming or not? This is your chance to meet a real, live unicorn."

"Okay, okay. Wait for us. We're coming with you, but I warn you, this had better be good," yelled Schubert, as he and his news hounds bounded over and joined Badger atop Nippy Nimbus.

Back at Twin Pines, Mr Bigfoot pulled off his big boots, rubbed his painful bunions and told his worried wife all about his traumatic day.

Outside, a pair of watchful eyes observed the scene inside. It was the news hound with the scarf and satchel, who had escaped Badger's Hypnotic Robotic spell, and followed Mr Bigfoot home.

Chapter Seven

"You'll have to jump from here. This is as low as I can go," grumbled Nippy.

Badger peered down warily. They were hovering above the treetops of the Enchanted Forest.

The news hounds were fidgety and nervous.

"I haven't seen any sign of this supposed unicorn yet," barked Schubert. "What are we doing on this stupid cloud anyway?"

"All in good time," said Badger. "The current problem is getting down from here. Do you have any suggestions?"

Schubert looked over the edge of the cloud. "Is your unicorn definitely down there?"

Badger nodded.

"Right, news hounds, form a ladder," their leader commanded.

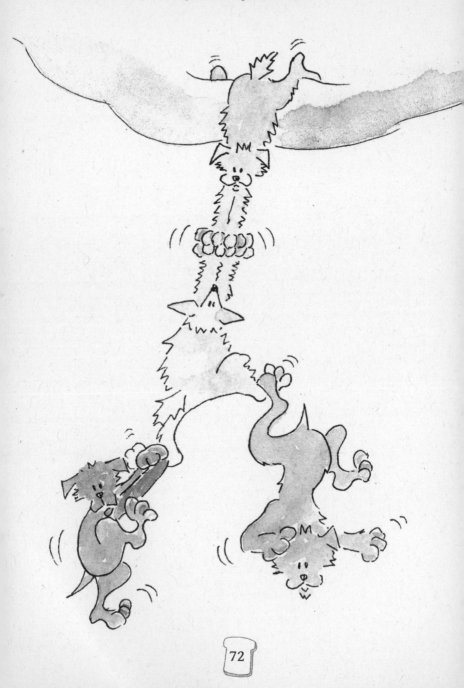

The news hounds looked at each other uneasily.

"*Now*, if you please!" ordered Schubert, "and tell me when you hit the ground. Then I will follow you."

Nippy Nimbus giggled. After many yelps, groans, bumps and bruises, they eventually landed on a pile of leaves.

"What about me?" shouted Badger, who was still looking nervously down from Nippy Nimbus.

"I thought big jumps would be your idea of fun in the snowboarding world," jeered Schubert.

Oh no, thought Badger, *I can't fly or ask 'Chief to parachute me down, or they'll see me and my magic won't be secret anymore. I need a bouncy bottom spell super quick.*

"What's keeping you? You're surely not frightened of a little leap, are you?" Schubert jibed.

"I'll be there in a moment. I just have to psyche myself up." Badger sighed.

He closed his eyes and muttered quietly:

"Blimey- climby, topsy-turvy,
Make the bottom soft and curvy.
With squishy landings when I fall
Let me bounce like a big beach ball."

He opened one eye and stepped off of the cloud.

"That's what they call 'blasting a dookie' in the snowboarding world," laughed one of the news hounds.

"What does that mean?" asked Schubert, as Badger got up and rubbed his tail.

"Falling really hard," said another news hound, still chuckling.

"Right, where now?" demanded Schubert. "Lead us to your unicorn!"

Badger strode forward and headed for the Crystal Cave where he knew his friend, Orlando, a most magnificent and majestic unicorn, was most likely to be found.

Back at Twin Pines, Mrs Bigfoot heard a sharp rap at the door.

"Goodness, Badger should know he doesn't need to knock," she tutted, wiping her hands on her apron to answer.

She opened the door smiling, but was met with an unfamiliar face. She tried to close the door quickly, but the stranger put his paw against it.

"Please don't be frightened" said the visitor softly. He wore a long scarf and carried a satchel. "My name is Hugo Gallant and I'm here to help."

When Badger, Schubert and the news hounds reached the dazzling entrance of the Crystal Cave, the Pupparazzi flashed their press passes, expecting automatic entry, but Badger pushed them away.

"There's no guest list here. Stand back and watch."

Badger cleared his throat and spoke very softly:

"Unicorn, unicorn, where do you hide?
Come to me now, and appear by my side.
Show these hounds your magic horn
And prove you're a real live unicorn."

They waited and held their breath. Then from around the side of the cave, a beautiful white creature, not unlike a horse, appeared.

The Pupparazzi gasped. Schubert swooned and Badger smiled.

"I'm so glad you could come," boomed Orlando boldly.

The Pupparazzi stepped back in awe. In front of them stood a huge, powerful, regal beast, with a shimmering horn in the middle of its forehead.

Oh boy, thought Schubert, quivering with excitement, *a real, live unicorn. This story is going to make me so famous, I'll sell newspapers galore.*

Suddenly, the unicorn spoke in a commanding tone:

"Now, I believe you wish to have a photo shoot. I'm ready if you are, gentlemen. Please stand in line."

The Pupparazzi reached automatically for their cameras. But all of their photographic equipment had been left behind at Pookamoa, in the Kora La, and Mr Bigfoot had now buried it deep in the Heralayan Mountain.

Schubert stepped forward and stood face to face with the unicorn. "What do you mean, stand in line?" he barked.

"Perhaps I should have explained. You lot *are* the photo shoot! My magic horn can do lots of things, including taking and then sharing photos across the universe. I know my fellow mythical creatures will want to know of your presence in our dimension. This is *big* news." The unicorn pointed its horn directly at Schubert and glared defiantly.

Schubert stuttered and spluttered and stood back, speechless. The news hounds cowered behind him. Badger chuckled as Orlando scanned them all with his magical horn and breathed in deeply.

Now Schubert and the Pupparazzi know what it feels like to be on the other side of the camera, thought Badger.

Chapter Eight

Hugo Gallant was seated by the fire enjoying a bowl of Mrs Bigfoot's heart-warming broth.

Mr and Mrs Bigfoot sat opposite, watching him nervously.

Hugo wiped his mouth with his napkin and sat back.

"That was utterly delicious. Thank you so much for your kind hospitality. Now, allow me to explain my reason for rapping rather rudely on your door, unannounced and uninvited."

At the Crystal Cave, Schubert and the news hounds had recovered quickly enough from the shock of seeing a real, live unicorn, but not from the horror of having no cameras to take pictures, or from the humiliation of being the focus of their own photo shoot. The air around them crackled with electricity as Orlando blasted a blinding blue light from his horn and uploaded the pictures to magic-mail.

"What now, boss?" asked the Pupparazzi together.

"Right" said Schubert sharply, "if we can't capture the creature on film, we'll need to capture it alive and take it back with us. That unicorn can't outwit us. We've got this!"

Schubert produced a rope lasso.

"This should work a treat," he added.

"Nice one, Mr Furdog," said the news hounds.

"But you can't. Orlando has never left this dimension. If he does, he'll die," gasped Badger.

"Nonsense!" barked Schubert. "He seems in fine fettle to me."

Orlando smiled.

"Don't worry, Badger. Let them try and catch me. This could be fun, and once I'm bored with the chase, I can always just zap them."

The unicorn turned on its hooves and ran.

Schubert and the news hounds followed immediately, shielding their eyes from the dazzling entrance. They sped after the unicorn, running clumsily. They bashed at the gleaming crystal stalactites in their way that hung from the cave roof, and scrabbled over stalagmites growing up from the ground. They bumped, banged and bumbled their way, chasing the nimble unicorn amongst the crystal structures.

Suddenly, one of the Pupparazzi got wedged between a pair of criss-cross stalagmites. He wailed in agony. The rest of the hounds halted to help their colleague.

"Leave him, or we'll lose the unicorn." yelled Schubert to the others.

Ahead, lay three possible avenues amidst the crystals.

The news hounds all stood in a line in confusion. "Which way do we go, boss?"

"This way," roared Schubert confidently as he caught a glimpse of the unicorn's tail heading down the left-hand path. They chased onwards through archways of crystal and chambers of light.

Badger knew his way around the cave, so was able to get ahead of them and wait.

Finally, Orlando reached the very back of the cave. There was nowhere else to run.

"Trapped you, have we?" panted Schubert, racing to catch up with his news hounds.

The unicorn stood facing them coolly.

Then everything seemed to happen at once.

As Schubert cast his rope lasso towards Orlando, Badger's neckerchief caught it in mid-air; Orlando's horn glowed and sprayed a fine mist of stun spray over the news hounds and Schubert. Then Badger bellowed an untried, but mischievous spell:

"Read all about it, or read it and weep,
For yours are the secrets that no one will keep.
Gibberish and claptrap you will now speak,
Until no one has faith in the stories you seek."

Schubert and the news hounds stood absolutely still like statues. 'Chief looped the lasso over them all and returned to Badger's neck. Orlando shook his mane in relief.

"I see your stun spray worked. Let's just hope my *Stuff and Nonsense* spell has worked as well," smiled Badger.

"Well done, Badger, and 'Chief too," said Orlando, "but I'm enjoying myself. Let's give them a taste of their own medicine again and take a look at magic-mail."

Orlando pointed his horn at the cave wall and beamed forth a brilliantly vivid image. Schubert and the Pupparazzi watched in horror as they saw a headline circling the world, then multiply and zoom around every planet in the universe. The words read:

SCHUBERT FURDOG AND THE PUPPARAZZI ARE A BUNCH OF NINCOMPOOPS!

In glorious technicolour, the accompanying picture showed Schubert and

his news hounds tied up and startled.

Orlando's stun spray was wearing off, but Schubert and the news hounds were still rather stunned by the mortifying spectacle on the screen.

"What do you think of my U.U.U. then, Badger?" asked Orlando proudly?

"Your Unicorn Universal Upload? That takes the World Wide Web into a new dimension. Epic!" smiled Badger.

"Exactly!" said the unicorn.

Schubert slumped in defeat. He had been outwitted by a mythical beast.

Back at Twin Pines, Mr Bigfoot was shaking his head vigorously.

"Not on your nellie! Never in a million years! We've spent our lives fleeing from the newspapers, and now you want to run a story on us?"

"You misunderstand me. I want *you* to tell *your* story, *your* way. I'm not from the *Paws of the World*. I'm from a much more well-regarded paper, the *Talking Tails*," said Hugo gently.

"I don't understand," said the Yeti.

"Schubert and the Pupparazzi want to depict you as a monster, Mr Bigfoot; a *thing*, to be hunted, captured or shot. They don't know the true story: that there is nothing to be afraid of; that you have a wife and a family; that you don't want to hurt anyone; and just want to be left in peace."

"I don't even have big feet, only bunions and big boots," sighed Mr Bigfoot.

"And layers upon layers of socks," added Mrs Bigfoot.

"Really? Oh, that's even better," said Hugo raising his eyebrows. "Well, that's a perfect human interest story."

"But we're *not* human Mr Gallant."

"Yes, of course. But the point is, if I write it up ... well, then it will destroy Schubert's story of you being *abominable* — it will totally spike it — and then you can go about your business without constantly looking over your shoulder. For instance, do your children play outdoors?"

Mr and Mrs Bigfoot shook their heads sadly.

"So, don't you owe it to them to take this chance and get rid of Schubert and his Pupparazzi once and for all?"

"But how can we be sure we can trust you?" said Mr Bigfoot suspiciously.

Hugo stood up on two paws, threw back his head and let out an almighty Yeti roar. Twin Pines shook with the vibration.

Mr and Mrs Bigfoot jumped back in alarm. Flossy and Bossie sped downstairs and stopped in their tracks, open-mouthed, when they saw the visitor.

"You see, I'm your kin. My great-great-great-grandfather was from these parts and married a huskimo who was here on holiday," Hugo smiled.

"What on earth is a huskimo?" asked Mrs Bigfoot, incredulous, pulling her children towards her.

"A huskimo is more commonly known as a huskie. My great-great-great-grandmother was a champion sled-dog racer. I only want to protect you, as I would my own family. *Now* do you believe that I only want what is best for you?"

Chapter Nine

Orlando sighed.

"Can I go, please?" asked the unicorn. "I'm really bored now. You can take it from here, Badger."

"Of course you can go now, Orlando," bowed the Mystical Mutt. "Thank you for showing this lot what it's like to have your name spread so widely and in such a shameful way."

"Anytime." Orlando winked, bowing in return.

The unicorn touched the tip of its magical horn to the ground and, in a flash, vanished.

Badger watched as the statues began to twitch, wriggle and squiggle. He heard a few groans and moans and then voices shouting a foreign mixed-up language.

"Heresway sisay hetsay nicornusay," yelled Schubert.

Heh heh, laughed Badger, *the stun spray may have worn off but my Stuff and Nonsense spell has worked a treat. They can only speak in baxy-waxy language now and forever more until I decide to break the spell.*

"Heresway sisay hetsay nicornusay?" asked Badger grinning "Do you mean 'where is the unicorn?'"

"Tupidsay nowboardingsay uttsmay?" barked Schubert, looking very puzzled.

"Yes, I can see why you'd call me a 'stupid snowboarding mutt'," giggled Badger, "but

I'm the only one who can get you out of here and home, so you'd best just do as I say now, and follow my lead."

Schubert snarled. Badger shrugged his shoulders and turned to leave. Schubert and the news hounds plodded wearily after him, to the cave entrance and back into the Enchanted Forest, with their lips sealed.

Badger stopped when they reached a clearing.

He closed his eyes. Sparkles of light appeared around him as he whispered his special cloud-charming spell:

"Give me a trumpet to call you here.
Wherever you are, may the sky be clear.
I miss your surly and grumpy play.
We need you, Nippy, and your cotton-wool
sleigh."

Suddenly, a shiny silver bugle dropped down in front of them. Before Schubert or the Pupparazzi could react, quick as a flash, Badger snatched it to his lips and blew out a fanfare. The Mystical Mutt looked hopefully into the sky above. Schubert and the news hounds peered upwards too.

Hugo had, at last, convinced Mr and Mrs Bigfoot that they should allow themselves to be interviewed by him. "I'm a believer in being able to speak the truth freely. That's why I wanted to be a journalist, and of course, I have to defend the right of the likes of Schubert to express their opinion too. His truth, however, is different from my truth, your truth or any truth. His reporting style is steeped in sensation, and all about whipping his readers into a frenzy of terror, and about making the lives of those he writes about utterly miserable. And this is all because he wants to sell headlines and newspapers. The fact is you are not hurting anyone," said Hugo.

"I agree with you about free speech, Mr Gallant. We try to teach our children to be honest. However, as you say, Mr Furdog is dealing in lies and portraying us as monsters, which we are not. So okay, we will do this interview for you," sighed Mr Bigfoot.

"Terrific! Thank you. First of all then, I need some pictures of you at home with your family. Now let's get you in position, please."

Flossy and Bossie wriggled mischievously on the sofa with Mr and Mrs Bigfoot standing behind, smiling in a typical family portrait. Hugo snapped away and showed them the pictures he had taken.

"I don't look my best in that one at all," winced Mrs Bigfoot.

"You look terrific, as always," smiled her husband.

"No problem. Let's take some more. I only want to use photographs that you are all

completely happy with," said Hugo kindly.
"Mrs Bigfoot, may I be so bold as to ask your
first name?"

"It's Betty. Betty Bigfoot," replied Mrs
Bigfoot

"Betty?" asked Hugo "So, you're Betty the
Yeti? Terrific!"

He clicked again.

"Right, now that's done, let's get the
interview started. I want you to be as

relaxed as possible, and you don't need to answer *anything* you don't feel comfortable with. Shall we begin with the fact that you do not, Mr Bigfoot, have big feet?" Hugo produced his notebook and pen, and they all settled down for a lively chat.

On the mountain, things were not well between Badger and his grumpy cloud.

"It's not like you to blow your own trumpet. So you think you can just click your paws and I'll come a-floating, do you, Badger?" moaned Nippy Nimbus, hovering above them all.

"Sorry to point out the obvious, Nippy, but that's exactly what you've done, thank you very much, except my paws didn't click. I just blew this bugle actually," Badger grinned.

"Okay, this is the last time today without a password. Jump up then," groaned the cloud.

Badger looked at Schubert playfully and said: "Do you think you could do that fancy thing with the dog ladder again? It's a bit too high to jump."

Schubert nodded reluctantly, afraid to speak, in case more gobbledygook came out and pointed to his news hounds to get into position and climb onto the cloud. As Badger, Schubert and the Pupparazzi drifted away on the cloud, Badger looked back to see Orlando's horn glowing brightly below.

Soon they were back at the top of the mountain. But how were they going to get back down to Pookamoa? The red carpet was buried somewhere underneath a recent snowfall and could not be seen.

Chapter Ten

Schubert and his news hounds gathered around Badger agape. The Mystical Mutt had untied his neckerchief, placed it flat on the snow-covered ground and was standing on it.

"C'mon, get on," said Badger.

Schubert shook his head vigorously.

"Unless you want to plough down on your paws, with the possibility of avalanches and not knowing what lies beneath the snow, then you need to trust me. Remember, I am a champion snowboarder, after all." Badger crossed his paws behind his back and hoped they'd never know the truth. "Now, even if you can all only get one paw on, please do it now," Badger instructed.

Schubert looked doubtfully at the tiny square of red-and-white polka dots.

"Look, I got you to the Enchanted Forest and the Crystal Cave, and I showed you a real, live unicorn, didn't I? You have to believe that I can get us all down quickly and unharmed. Just relax and chill out," said Badger calmly.

Schubert breathed a heavy sigh, and placed a paw on the neckerchief. He beckoned for the others to do the same.

Badger closed his eyes and said: *"'Chief, 'Chief, my safety advisor, please become an improviser."*

The small square of fabric began to grow in width, length and density. Within a few blinks, Badger, Schubert and the news hounds were all aboard a snazzy sheet of gleaming fibreglass.

"This is the biggest snowboard I've ever seen," gasped Badger. "Awesome, 'Chief! Now let's just go for a cruiser-run." The board began to slide forwards softly before gathering speed.

"No need to show off with any misty flips or spaghetti airs," yelled Badger nervously.

"Hold on everyone!"

The snowboard raced further on down the mountain, cutting through the powder with increasing pace. They were nearly at the bottom.

Suddenly Badger shrieked and pointed his paw in terror. "Whoa! Watch out, 'Chief! Massive death cookie ahead."

A huge frozen snowball sat smack bang in the centre of their run.

But it was too late for 'Chief to stop.

"This has been a delight, Mr and Mrs Bigfoot. Your children are amazing, and I'm so proud that you have given me your permission to run this story," smiled Hugo back at Twin Pines.

"And you definitely think this will stop Schubert and his Pupparazzi hounding us?" asked Mr Bigfoot.

"Without a doubt! You will cease to be newsworthy, *especially* when they discover that you don't actually have big feet. They can hardly call you 'Bigfoot' after that revelation. The children will be able to play outdoors again. You can enjoy your daily forage, and Mrs Bigfoot, you will be able to go to Miss Monaghan's for your weekly shop again."

Mrs Bigfoot smiled happily.

"I know someone round here who won't be very happy though," grinned Mr Bigfoot. "Shifty Sid."

"Shifty Sid? Is he one of the news hounds?" asked Hugo ."I think I've met him."

"He's not one of the Pupparazzi, but he's our local wheeler-dealer. His entire trade is based on selling Bigfoot merchandise to Schubert and his news hounds to take back home as souvenirs."

"Oh well, for every winner, there's usually a loser. It's not your fault. You've given him a good trade for a long time. Now, will Miss Monaghan's have wi-fi? I really need to type up your interview and p-mail it through to the newspaper," asked Hugo.

"Yes, she's got a telegraph pole for very important p-mails, if she's open. Will you send us a copy when it runs?" asked Mrs Bigfoot.

"Of course. I'll send you several, so Flossy and Bossie can have their own copies too."

"Will you come back and see us if you are bound this way again?" asked Mr Bigfoot.

"Indeed, and that might be sooner than you think. I somehow feel like I belong here," said Hugo with a faraway look in his eyes.

Mr and Mrs Bigfoot and Flossy and Bossie waved their visitor off and closed the door.

They all breathed a huge sigh of relief.
Maybe their lives could be normal again
after all.

Badger, Schubert and the news hounds were
tossed up into the air, as the snowboard
came to an abrupt halt, with its nose dug
deep into the gigantic snowball. They
plummeted to the ground face-first in
the snow, and began to roll ... and roll.
When the rolling balls of snow-covered fur
eventually came to a stop at the bottom, all
was very still.

When Hugo arrived at Miss Monaghan's
shack, the shutter slammed down
immediately. He rapped politely on the edge
of the counter.

"Ahem, hello, Miss Monaghan? Please can
you open the shutter? I desperately need
to make use of your wi-fi. It's very urgent.
I must send my story to my newspaper, *The
Talking Tails.*

There was a sharp snort, followed by
silence.

"I'm on a deadline, Miss Monaghan. Please can you open up?" pleaded Hugo.

"No chance there, mate," said a voice from behind him. "Miss Monaghan will not entertain strangers, especially not your sort."

Hugo turned around to see a swaggering fox emerge from an underground den.

"What do you mean my *sort?*" sniffed Hugo, slightly miffed.

"You know ... dodgy newspaper types, headline hunters," said the fox coolly, as he hammered on the shutter.

Hugo blustered and spluttered, as Miss

Monaghan's shutter flew up.

"Shifty Sid, what can I do for you?" asked the goat from behind the counter.

"I'm after some of that raspberry and Brussels-sprout lemonade to fizzle my vim, Miss Monaghan. I've also got a new range of finest Heralayan Mountain mugs to show you. I'll do you a deal," said Sid, rubbing his paws together.

"Why will you serve him, but not me?" asked Hugo in confusion.

"We are a very tight-knit community here, youngster, and we don't like the likes of you coming in and telling untruths about us to the rest of the world. So no, the wi-fi is not available, and I'm not open for business. Goodbye. Shifty, come in by the secret door."

Shifty Sid turned and blew a raspberry at Hugo and scurried round the back of the kiosk.

The shutter slammed shut again.

Hugo stood, bewildered, not knowing quite what to do next.

Suddenly, two big paws grabbed Hugo's shoulders. He turned around in alarm.

"It's only me, Hugo," grinned Mr Bigfoot. "I'm on my way to catch some fish. Can you not get in? Is Miss Monaghan closed?"

Hugo sighed. "Well, she is and she isn't. She's open for Shifty Sid, who is inside, but totally closed for me. I need to get your story sent through now before Schubert and his Pupparazzi do their worst."

Mr Bigfoot chuckled and slapped him on the back. "Leave it to me, Hugo. You'll get your story delivered on time."

The shutter squeaked open a notch and two pairs of eyes peered through.

"Do you know him then?" asked Shifty.

"Of course! He's practically family. Now, Miss Monaghan, will you please open your shutter fully, and let Hugo use your wi-fi, so that he can send his story? And we'll both have some lemonade too please, while you're at it."

The shutter opened completely, Miss Monaghan laid tumblers of lemonade across

the counter, and handed Hugo a piece of paper with the wi-fi password.

"You can have ten minutes for free on me," said the goat graciously, "Any friend of Mr Bigfoot's is a friend of mine."

Hugo sent his story in a jiffy, and gulped down the delicious lemonade. He also advised Shifty that his reign as the Bigfoot merchandise king may be coming to an end, but that he had a contact on the banks of Loch Ness, if he wanted to expand his business.

As Mr Bigfoot headed off on his fish-catching jaunt, Sid was already sketching out ideas for Loch Ness Monster pencil cases and looking forward to a trip to Scotland where the air was cold ... but not as cold as the Heralayan Mountain.

He was also feeling smug about an order from Miss Monaghan for forty-four Heralayan tourist mugs. He left her shack with a spring in his step, because Miss Monaghan hadn't noticed that ten of the mugs had their handles on the inside.

Chapter Eleven

Hugo whistled happily between burps, as he trekked towards the bottom of the mountain. He wanted one last look at Pookamoa before he left. He had been in luck bumping into Mr Bigfoot outside Miss Monaghan's shack. The Internet connection had worked, he had sent his p-mail and his story was set to run the next day.

He suddenly stopped whistling, as he came upon a peculiar collection of large oddly shaped snowballs.

How odd, he thought as he was sure he saw one of them move slightly. *It must be the breeze.*

Then one of the snowballs jiggled, and another wobbled. Hugo tip-toed closer and stepped back in fright, as a paw punched out from inside the largest snowball. Another

paw thrust out from the other side, and
then a head poked out from the top. It was
Badger the Mystical Mutt.

"It's you, the champion snowboarder!
Thank goodness. I thought this mountain
actually did have abominable snowballs or
something," said Hugo relieved.

Badger pointed to the row of other
snowballs beside him and said: "You're not

wrong. Look who's with me."

Schubert shook himself free of his snowball, and one by one all the news hounds did the same. Badger touched his neck, which felt very damp. His neckerchief had returned, but it was soaking wet after its snow dip.

"Is everyone okay? No broken bones?" asked Badger apprehensively.

The dogs looked a bit frazzled and dazed, but otherwise they were all fine.

"I told you I'd get you down the mountain safely, didn't I?" said Badger smiling. "That was maybe not *quite* the way I'd intended, but we're here now."

Hugo chuckled at the bedraggled news hounds. Badger turned to Hugo, remembering that he'd seen him before.

"Hang on! Aren't *you* one of the news hounds too? The one with the scarf and the satchel?" He pointed. "Why didn't you come with us?"

"Aha, because I know more than you think, I know who *you* really are, Badger the

Mystical Mutt. And I wouldn't risk my life or limbs, because I also know you're definitely *not* a champion snowboarder!"

Badger looked at Hugo suspiciously.

"Besides which, I had other, more important business to attend to," added Hugo. "Allow me to introduce myself. I'm Hugo Gallant, one of the few remaining, all-round good guys."

As Badger and Hugo shook paws, Schubert growled: "Hereisway idsday ousyay ogsay?"

Hugo looked at Badger.

"Shall I translate for you, Schubert?" Badger giggled.

Schubert nodded crossly.

"He said, 'where did you go?' I'm afraid they've all got a bit of a language barrier now, where they can only speak in baxy-waxy."

"Oh dear," chortled Hugo, standing eye to eye with Schubert. "You'll have a tricky time getting anyone to believe you've seen a Yeti then."

"Hereisway idsday ousyay ogsay?" repeated Schubert furiously.

"Oh, I know that one! So, where did *I* go? Well, I went to meet Mr Bigfoot. I got a great interview, telling the story from his and his family's viewpoint, and some great photographs too." Hugo patted his satchel. "I've sent the story straight through to the *Talking Tails* and it should run tomorrow."

Schubert pawed the ground angrily.

"But Schubert," continued Hugo, "you were ready to portray them as monsters and were making their lives a misery. If you'd run the sensational story, there would have been hordes of hunters here, determined to capture, hurt or wipe out the Bigfoots. I respect your right to your opinion, but there's no way I could let you tell such untruths. So, I told a little fib about wanting to be your deputy, or you would never have let me join you on this trip."

Schubert seethed, then shouted sharply to his news hounds: "Etsgay hetsay atchelsay!"

"What's he saying?" asked Hugo, but before Badger could answer, the news hounds launched themselves upon them both. As they lay pinned to the ground by the Pupparazzi, Schubert slid quietly away with Hugo's satchel.

"He said, 'get the satchel', and now I think he's got it," said Badger sadly.

Mr Bigfoot was having a successful trawl for fish when he spotted Schubert on the other side of the river. He had Hugo's satchel and was rummaging inside.

This isn't right, thought Mr Bigfoot, *Hugo would never betray us like this, not when he's one of us. There's something fishy going on here, and it's not my catch of the day.*

Quietly, Mr Bigfoot slunk into the shadows of the trees with his net and double-backed down the embankment, until he could wade across unnoticed.

When he reached the other side, he crept along until he was behind Schubert. Stealthily, he edged closer, and cast his net directly over the *Paws of the World* editor.

Schubert jolted and, in his shock, dropped Hugo's camera into the fast-flowing river.

Chapter Twelve

Mr Bigfoot hoisted Schubert in his net over his shoulder, and carried him back to the others.

"Back off you lot, or your leader might just be going for a very long swim," roared Mr Bigfoot. Schubert trembled inside the netting.

The news hounds released their grip on Hugo and Badger.

"I'm afraid your camera has gone, Hugo. This nitwit dropped it into the river. I'm sorry," said

Mr Bigfoot, brushing the snow from his fur.

Hugo smiled. "I can easily get another camera, Mr Bigfoot, and I've already sent the photographs that you approved through to the paper, so everything is fine."

"What do you want me to do with this?" asked the Yeti, pointing at Schubert, writhing about in the net.

"Oh, let him go. There's nothing he can do now to hurt us. He can't even string a sentence together, let alone write a story for a newspaper," said Hugo generously.

Mr Bigfoot opened his net, and Schubert fell to the ground with a thud.

"Now," said Badger, "as your dastardly plan has backfired, can I suggest you and your Pupparazzi go home and leave us in peace?"

"Because if you don't," warned Hugo, "Mrs Bigfoot makes a tasty broth with whatever Mr Bigfoot brings home from his foraging, and I suspect you'd be a tough chew. Quite gristly."

Mr Bigfoot licked his lips.

Schubert and the news hounds scarpered faster than the quickest thing ever.

The next day, the story ran as Hugo had promised it would in the *Talking Tails*. It showed Mr Bigfoot, Mrs Bigfoot, Flossy and Bossie as lovable Yetis, who wanted a quiet life and world peace. Most importantly, the piece revealed that Mr Bigfoot did not have big feet. The newspaper had also set up a charity to protect endangered and hunted species throughout the world. The article in the *Talking Tails* was very vague geographically, and because Hugo had interviewed them so cleverly, every question had been answered, and there was nothing left for anyone to wonder about.

Unusually, Miss Monaghan's shutter stayed open, while Badger shopped for the ingredients for a very important spell. There was just one more thing he had to do for the Bigfoots before he left the Heralayan Mountain. When he returned to the kitchen

of Twin Pines, he put all the ingredients into a large cauldron and stirred the mixture three times clockwise, and twice anti-clockwise. Sparkles of light appeared around him and his eyebrows twitched as he uttered the magical rhyme:

"Peppermint leaves on a lavender breeze,
Rosemary flowers to add to its ease,
Oil from the tea tree with allium onions,
Mix up together to soothe Bigfoot bunions."

The spell worked a treat and Mr Bigfoot

was, at last, bunion-free.

The Bigfoot family were forever grateful to Badger, although Mrs Bigfoot admitted that she had had her doubts at the beginning, as to whether Badger's magic would be strong enough to solve their

problem. Although Schubert and his news hounds had left the Heralayan Mountain, Badger decided to release them from his *Stuff and Nonsense* baxy-waxy spell, but only up to a point. If Schubert ever mentioned the words "Bigfoot" or "Yeti", he would immediately return to speaking utter gibberish for the rest of the day.

Mr Bigfoot and Badger returned to the place where he thought he'd parked his Wim-Wim for a Wowser to Wind the Weather up on a Wet Day, but could not find it. Luckily, Mr Bigfoot knew the terrain inside out. He pointed to a patch where the top of the Wim-Wim was just about peeking through. Mr Bigfoot burped some extra big burps for Badger's Haboba juice fuel, and waved the Mystical Mutt farewell.

Badger dusted off the rest of the snow from his Wim-Wim, got inside and started the engine. It was time to go home.

Another badgical-magical job well done, he thought, feeling very pleased with himself.

As he defrosted the dashboard and

demisted the glass, he looked around. It was good to be back in his favourite travelling machine.

And that was when he spotted another envelope.

Epilogue

After Badger left the Heralayan Mountain, Shifty Sid shut up shop and travelled to the banks of Loch Ness, where he opened a kiosk selling Nessie souvenirs.

Flossy and Bossie thrived playing outside and making friends.

Mrs Bigfoot enjoyed her weekly chats with Miss Monaghan and, as a result, usually forgot what she had gone into the shop to buy.

Miss Monaghan's shutter was mostly open, except for when she was meeting Billy, her new, best pal, from the other side of the Kora La, down the Velvet Road.

On the other side of the world, none of Schubert's colleagues believed anything he had to say about Bigfoot or a Yeti, mainly because they couldn't understand baxy-waxy. They never did believe that he'd met a real, live unicorn. The headlines rang with the fact the great Schubert Furdog had lost out on his big Bigfoot story to the *Paws of the World's* biggest rival: Hugo Gallant and the *Talking Tails* newspaper.

Mr Furdog became the headline he had craved, especially because he kept insisting he'd met a unicorn. Eventually, he got a job, writing a weekly review column on pooper-scoopers.

The Unicorn Universal Upload on Schubert went viral, and magical creatures throughout the cosmos felt so sorry for him that they set up a charity on his behalf. It was called the *Foolish Furdog Fund*.

Hugo decided the newspaper world was no longer what he wanted to do with his life. He moved to the Heralayan Mountain, built a cabin quite close to Twin Pines, and traced his family tree, making full use of Miss Monaghan's Internet facility. He then wrote a bestseller, but no one except Badger, Mr and Mrs Bigfoot, Flossy, Bossie,

Shifty Sid and Miss Monaghan knew of the famous author's whereabouts.

And now completely bunion-free, Mr Bigfoot ran his first half-marathon ... just because he could.

ALSO PUBLISHED BY THE LUNICORN PRESS

Badger the Mystical Mutt
ISBN: 978-0-9569640-0-7

**Badger the Mystical Mutt
and the Barking Boogie**
ISBN: 978-0-9560640-1-4

**Badger the Mystical Mutt
and the Crumpled Capers**
ISBN: 978-0-9569640-2-1

**Badger the Mystical Mutt
and the Daydream Drivers**
ISBN: 978-0-9569640-4-5

**Badger the Mystical Mutt
and the Enchanting Exchange**
ISBN: 978-0-9569640-5-2

**Badger the Mystical Mutt
and the Flying Fez**
ISBN: 978-0-9569640-6-9

www.badgerthemysticalmutt.com